and Jimmy Durante and Helena Rubinstein for their help. Not to mention Mr. Tibor and LuLu and Alexander and my mother Sara and the mean lean Dean Lubensky machine. But finally and mostly, this book is dedicated to the delirious and hilarious Slutsky family, with loving memory of Yona.

and Igor Stravinsky and Danny Kaye I want to thank for this book, up the name Schoenfeld for thinking K-k-kika my sister I want to thank laughs last. He who laughs last nuthin. Nuthin equals nuthin from

This is a New York Review Book, published by The New York Review of Books, 435 Hudson Street, Suite 300, New York City, NY, 10014, The United States of America, www.nyrb.com ISBN 978-1-68137-170-2 Available as an ebook; ISBN 978-1-68137-171-9

Printed in the United States of America on acid-free paper Designed by M&CO 2 4 6 8 10 9 7 5 3 1 First published in 1990 A catalog record for this book is available from the Library of Congress

MAX MAKES A MILLION

BY MAIRA KALMAN

THE NEW YORK REVIEW

CHILDREN'S COLLECTION

Call me Max.

Max the dreamer.

Max the poet.

Max the dog.

My dream is to live in Paris.

To live in Paris and be a p^{o}e^t.

Paris.
The city of dreams.
The city of lights.
The city of love.

But do you think it is easy for a dog to pack a small brown suitcase, put on a beret, and hop on a plane? Ha! Plane tickets cost money. Mazuma, shekels, semolians. I have none. Because no one wants to buy my book. I'm flat broke.

Bone dry.

But someday,
fat families and
skinny families
around the world
will be reading my poems.
And laughing, and crying.
I feel it in my bones.

I want to say, before anything,
that dreams
are very important.

I live in New York City. That crazy quivering wondering wild city. A city like an enormous orchestra. A bebop city. Every-one playing music that screeches and slides into my ears. Everyone singing a different song. Everyone running a different way. All day, All night.

A jumping jazzy city. Tall people. Short people. Plaid people. Carrying boxes. Carrying chairs. Traffic. Towers. A shimmering stimmering triple-decker sandwich kind of city. Wow. New York. Bow Wow Wow.

I live with Ida and Morris Stravinsky in the spacious Stravinsky apartment. Morris has a ladies' shoe store. Stravinsky Shoes. Every day he goes down to his store and shows women different shoes. Pumps. Sandals. Slippers. Mules. Morris and his assistant Laura are designing shoes for the Queen of Sheba, who must be a very fussy woman, because every time a customer makes Morris crazy he says, "Who do you think you are, the Queen of Sheba?"

Meanwhile, across town, Ida is taking tango lessons with Maurice Chagall.

He has a big black shiny pompadour on his head and tiny shiny pointy shoes on his feet.

Morris and Ida don't have any children.
But they have me, Max.
And they start to cry every time
I bring up the subject of
moving to Paris.
They will have to face the facts.
There is an old Chinese proverb that says
parents must give their children two things,
roots and wings.   I have the roots.
        Now I want the wings.

Every morning I walk
downtown to my studio.
I pass the Gizmo Gallery.
I pass the Venus Beauty Salon
and Dance School. I daydream
and stroll and scribble
in my notebook. And every day
I pause on the corner of
Salami and Pastrami Street
and tape a poem on the wall.

People can stop
and read my poems
and then go on
their merry way.

I reach my studio,
the place I write.
I share my studio
with Bruno, my best friend.
Bruno is an artist.
He paints invisible paintings.

I met Bruno in the garden of the
Museum of Incredibly Modern Art.
He was holding a very
strange umbrella.
Maybe he thinks
the rain is invisible.

Ha!

Some people say,
"That Bruno is crazy."
But Bruno is
no crybaby.
He just keeps
working on   the ideas in his head.

If I didn't mention before,
I should mention now.
This book is about dreamers.
Wishful thinkers.
Dreamy blinkers.
Crazy nuts.

I go to my desk. A writer must write. I close my eyes, say the first three things I see, and write a poem.

Mrs. Hoogenschmidt

Fish

Mr. Hoogenschmidt

Saxophone

Nose

Glasses

It was on a **sunny summer** day that I met

Mrs.
Hoo
gen
schmidt
wearing
a
fish
on
her
head.

Mr. Hoogenschmidt
was walking
on his hands carrying an umbrella

dizzy fella

The doorbell rang.
It was Baby Henry who owns
Baby Henry's Candy Shop.
Baby Henry travels to Turkey for
Turkish Taffy and to Cairo
for Caramel Camels.
Now he was having a candy dilemma.
"I need your advice," he said.
"Try these lemon drops from Nice.
Are they nice?" "Nice," I said.
"Twice nice," said Bruno.
"Good that it's nice," said Baby Henry.

I closed my eyes
while the candy lay
on my tongue.

Lemon groves. Full moon.
Sylvia's yellow dress.

I want to say
that wonderful ideas
can come from anywhere.
Sometimes you make a mistake,
or break something, or lose a hat, and the next
thing you know, you get a great idea. My idea was to eat.

Bruno and I left the studio. Walking to lunch we passed the door of the mysterious twins Otto and Otto
and their two dogs
Otto and Otto.

Tacked onto the quatro Otto door is a note that toots in total rudeness and which I reproduce in toto:

Bruno and Marlene are in love.
Did I mention that when
Bruno met Marlene he stopped
painting invisible paintings for
one week and painted only Marlene.

We reach the
Domino Luncheonette.
Marlene is waiting.
Marlene is a scientist.

She is studying gravity, which is why we
are stuck to the ground and not flying
off in all directions. Our waiter's
name is Marcello. He is an
architect. But no one will
live in his houses. He
only wants to build
houses that
are upside
down.

Marlene is worried that in a
house like that her skirt would
fall over her face and
she would be embarrassed.
"Wear pants, Marlene," says Bruno.

Walking back to the studio

we pass Princess Lenina

and her faithful horse Rex.

We pass Mr. Van Tiegham.

He is a musician.

He plays his drumsticks

on the garbage cans,

lampposts,

metal doors,

and building walls.

We watch as he disappears

down the street

hammering

and bangering

his zigzag

city song.

Ha!

I am back in my chair
writing up a storm
when what should ring
but the phone. Ha!
It's Leon Kampinsky,
my agent. Do you know
what an agent does?
He smokes a cigar, takes your
writing, tries to sell it,
never does, and gets 15%.
That's what an agent does.
"Leon, what is it?" I ask.
"It's happened, Max. I did it.
I sold your book.
For a million dollars!
They love it, Max.
You're going to dance
on the roofs of that city
you're dying to go to.
Lucky fellow. Max.
You've got it made."

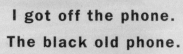

I got off the phone.
The black old phone.

Someone was going to print my book.
Someone was going to sell my book.
Someone was going to buy my book.

I couldn't talk.
I couldn't think.
I couldn't breathe.

The world was a fuzzy kind place.
The world was O.K.
Not just O.K. but A.O.K.
Bruno and I danced around.
Then I rushed uptown
to tell Morris and Ida.

They were
having a
party that night.
A musicale. A soirée.
I was going to recite my
poems. When I came home Ida
was frantic. "Quick, Max, start
making trays of canapés. Start
mixing martinis." "There's
something I have to tell you,
Ida." "Later, Max. Later. We
have guests coming. I have
to get dressed." I filled
platters with pomegranates
and figs. Bowls of olives
and baskets of tangerines.
My feet were rubbery.
My head was hot.
This was too much.
Too much for a
dog to bear.

The guests started arriving.

In walked Ivan Kazlinsky,
the arch rival of Leon Kampinsky.

"Ah, Max,"
sneered Ivan,
"still writing those
stupid little poems
that nobody likes?
Bring me a drink,
why don't you."
I was ready to rip the
pointy beard right off
his face. I was ready
to give his ugly pants
a bite so big, he would
be wearing shorts.
But instead I looked him
in the eye and said "Ha!"

And I secretly vowed
that Ivan Kazlinsky
would get his
terrible just desserts.

The party was a blur of perfume, silk dresses, and laughing voices. Ida said, "My dear friends. Would you kindly take your seats. We are ready."

It was mad. First cousin Etta swung on a trapeze with her husband Little Socco.

Then Rupert Mondasco played the bagpipes so hard they exploded, sending Helena Rubinstein's false eyelashes flying off her face. Bruno showed his paintings and Princess Lenina bought them all. "I love to see all this invisible stuff," the Princess explained.

Finally Marlene got up to explain gravity. "You see" she said, tossing three lemon pies into the air. "What goes up, m u s t come down."

And we all watched as the three lemon pies plopped, flopped, and dropped onto Ivan Kazlinsky's hairy horrified head.

Ha!
Ha!
Ha Ha!

It was my turn.
I shivered with fear
and excitement
and began to read:

I'm **gaga**
for a **saga**
of Ali **Baba**
and his forty **robbas.**

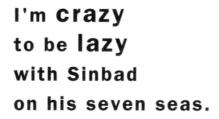

I'm **crazy**
to be **lazy**
with Sinbad
on his seven seas.

I want to dance
the **kazatski**
until I **plotski,**
and sing like a **boid**
on toity-toid and **toid**

Call me Max.
That lucky dog
with my dream shoes on

My life began
when I was **born.**
Hold the phone
I'll eat some **corn.**

Call me Max
that lucky dog.
With dream shoes
on my **feet.**
The world keeps
turning.
My shoes are **yearning**
to tapdance down
a lucky **street.**

The room was silent.
Then they all started to applaud.
"Max," they cried, "you are a
wunderdog, you are the funniest.
You are the greatest."

Dearest people,
How can I thank you.

This is the day
I have been waiting for
all my life. I am off.

Off to Paris to follow my dreams.
Be brave, Ida and Morris.
We will meet again
in that starry-eyed city.
You know I have always
lived by my dreams.
And now they have come true.
Roots and wings.
Roots and wings.
I've got to go,
Daddy-o.

So long.
Farewell.
Good-bye.

Ha!